# KEAKA
## and the
# LILIKO'I VINE

## By Donivee Martin Laird
## Illustrated by Carol Jossem

Barnaby Books  Honolulu, Hawaii

**Also By Barnaby Books:**

*The Three Little Hawaiian Pigs and the Magic Shark*
*Wili Wai Kula and the Three Mongooses*
*'Ula Li'i and the Magic Shark*

Published by:
Barnaby Books—a partnership
3290 Pacific Heights Road
Honolulu, Hawaii 96813

Printed and bound in Hong Kong under the
direction of:
Mandarin Offset

ISBN 0-940350-10-6

Third Printing, 1987.

# MAHALO TO OUR KEIKI

## KALA & KAKAIO

## LEA, IOKEPA, & AKAMU

## PRONUNCIATION GUIDE

The 12 letters in the Hawaiian alphabet are:
A, E, H, I, K, L, M, N, O, P, U, W

*consonants*
H, K, L, M, N, P are pronounced as in English
W is usually pronounced as V

*vowels*

A like a in farm
E like e in set
I like y in pretty

O like o in hold
U like oo in soon

*plural*
As there is no S in Hawaiian, the plural is formed by word usage or the addition of another word such as nā to the sentence.

On the island of Hawaii there is a hot dry place called the Ka'u Desert. It is not a desert of camels and sand. It is a desert of lava flows, dried grasses, and twisted kiawe trees. The young lava flows are black, and shine and twinkle in the sun. The old lava flows are gray and covered with tiny plants trying to grow.

Along the rocky shore, where the desert and sea meet, there was once the smallest and poorest village in all Hawaii. It wasn't much of a village. There were only a few houses, a dusty road, and on the black sand beach, several old canoes. At the edge of the village lived a widow and her son, Keaka.

They were poorer than the rest of the villagers. In order to eat, Keaka and his mother had to gather most of their food from along the shore and from their small garden. Keaka was too young to fish with the men in the canoes. Sometimes, though, the fishermen had a good catch and shared the extras with him.

Each morning, Keaka and the other village children set out to fish from the slippery rocks. Holding tightly to their poles, they threw their baited hooks far out into the surf and hoped the fish would bite. They searched the small pools, collecting crab, 'opihi, wana, and limu. And always they carefully kept out of the way of the huge waves which pounded the shore and washed over the lava.

One summer, after weeks without even a sprinkle of rain, the gardens in the village were dry. There was nothing fresh to eat. Keaka and his friends had picked food off the rocks until the rocks were nearly bare. Again and again the fishermen returned in their canoes empty-handed. The people of the village were hungry and worried.

Keaka's mother put a plate of dried fish and boiled sweet potato on the table. "This is all we have to eat," she said in a sad, tired voice.

"I will go far down the coast today," said Keaka. "For sure I will find plenty fish, wana, and 'opihi."

But, Keaka returned home that evening, tired and discouraged, with only a couple of fish and a small sack of limu. The fishermen too returned with just a few fish. And Keaka's mother had found only two bananas in the garden.

"We need money to buy food," said Keaka's mother. "You will have to sell Kūnānā."

"Oh mother no, not Kūnānā!" cried Keaka. He was proud of his large black and white goat. Kūnānā was the handsomest goat in the district.

"What else can we do my son?" asked his mother, sadly.

Keaka tried to think of another way for them to get food or money. No ideas came to him. His mother was right. Kūnānā must be sold.

Trying hard not to cry, Keaka tied a rope around his goat's neck.

Slowly they started up the dusty road on the long walk to town.

They had gone many miles when Keaka noticed something under a large tree. He walked closer and saw a man beside a small fruit stand. Where did he come from?

The thin man was dressed in red and wore a narrow lei of red feathers around his hat. He smiled and beckoned to Keaka. "Where are you going with that goat?" he asked in a musical voice.

"Up mauka. To town. To sell him," answered Keaka.

"So you are going to sell that handsome animal, are you?" asked the man with interest. "He is really too fine for you to sell. Have you ever thought about trading him?"

"Trading him for what?" wondered Keaka.

"Well," said the man slowly. "I have something quite valuable and wonderful right here." He reached into his pocket, brought out a small red bundle, and carefully began unwrapping it. Finally, he held it out for Keaka to see.

Shining in the sun were four black seeds.

"Liliko'i seeds!" exclaimed Keaka. "You think I would trade Kūnānā for seeds?" He turned to walk away.

"They are magic," said the man quietly.

Keaka stopped. "What did you say?" he asked, looking back.

"Magic," said the man in a smooth voice. "Very special magic . . . but, if you are not interested . . ." He began to wrap the seeds up again. Very carefully and very slowly he folded the red material over and over.

Keaka took a step closer. Suddenly it made him sad not to see the seeds gleaming in the bright sun.

"Wait," he cried. "Don't put them away."
The man's long thin fingers unwrapped the seeds once more and held them out for Keaka to see. Keaka stared and a soft singing voice said, "Their magic is very powerful and you can have all four of them for your goat."

Keaka smiled and without even knowing why, he made up his mind to trade. "All right," he said firmly. "You can have my goat." He handed the rope to the man and tenderly took the piece of red cloth with the twinkling seeds lying on it. Then carefully rewrapping them, he put the seeds deep in his pocket and hurried home to tell his mother the good news.

Now we all know that mothers are sometimes not as excited as we are about the wonderful things we bring home. This was definitely the case with Keaka's mother. She was not at all happy to see the magic seeds. In fact, she was very upset. "You foolish boy," she said in a voice growing louder. "You traded Kūnānā for four worthless liliko'i seeds?"

"But they are magic seeds," said Keaka, beginning to wonder if he had done the right thing.

"Magic seeds!" scoffed his mother. "There is no such thing as magic. Someone tricked you. Now what are we going to do? No food, no money, no goat. All we have are four liliko'i seeds." Keaka's mother grabbed the seeds and threw them as hard as she could. They flew out the window on to an old lava flow where they bounced and sparkled and rolled around until they slipped through a crack. Down they fell, landing on a patch of cool earth far under the rock.

   Keaka and his mother went to bed that
night feeling sad and wondering how they were
going to live.

While they slept, the moon shone on the still land and sent its moonbeams
down between the chunks of lava to touch the magic seeds. Slowly, ever so
slowly, the seeds began to swell until their black shells split open. There inside
were the beginnings of tiny green vines.

The vines uncurled and wound together. They reached and stretched and grew until they peeped out of a crevice in the lava and were one huge vine. The village slept and only a mouse cleaning his whiskers saw the vine continue to grow in the moonlight. He watched its tip disappear into the clouds.

Just as the morning sun was about to jump out of the ocean, Keaka woke up. He was hungry and wanted something to eat. At the door he stopped and stared.

"Mother!" he yelled in a loud, squeaking voice. "Come! Look! The seeds were magic!"

His mother hurried to the door. Her mouth and eyes opened wide. She was much too amazed to speak.

"I'm going up," said Keaka.

His mother was still so astonished that she forgot to say, "You shouldn't." Or, "It may be dangerous." Or even, "Be careful." So, up, up, up went Keaka. He climbed higher and higher and still higher until his head disappeared into the thick white clouds.

When at last he popped through the top of the cloud, Keaka found himself in a bright sunny world. There were flowers, trees, birds, and even a house, all made of white clouds. And scattered here and there were fantastic fluffy shapes.

A smooth path led to the house. Keaka decided to see who lived there. Bravely he walked up to the door and knocked.

A voice called, "I'm coming. Oh dear. I'm coming."

The door opened and there stood the largest woman Keaka had ever seen. She was muttering, "Oh dear, oh dear," and wringing her hands. She glanced around and didn't see anyone. As she shut the door, she looked down and there was Keaka.

"Oh dear," she exclaimed in a loud voice that made Keaka tremble. "Oh dear, it is a boy." She bent down and looked into Keaka's face and said, very loudly, "Go away boy. If my husband catches you, he will chew you all the way down to your manamana wāwae." (Keaka's toes began to shiver fearfully.)

As the woman spoke, a noise rumbled out from among the clouds.

"Oh dear. Oh dear," said the woman rapidly. "It is too late. What shall I do? My husband is coming. Oh dear. Quickly, quickly you must hide." As she spoke, she pulled Keaka into the house. "There isn't time," she cried closing the door, shoving Keaka behind her long skirt.

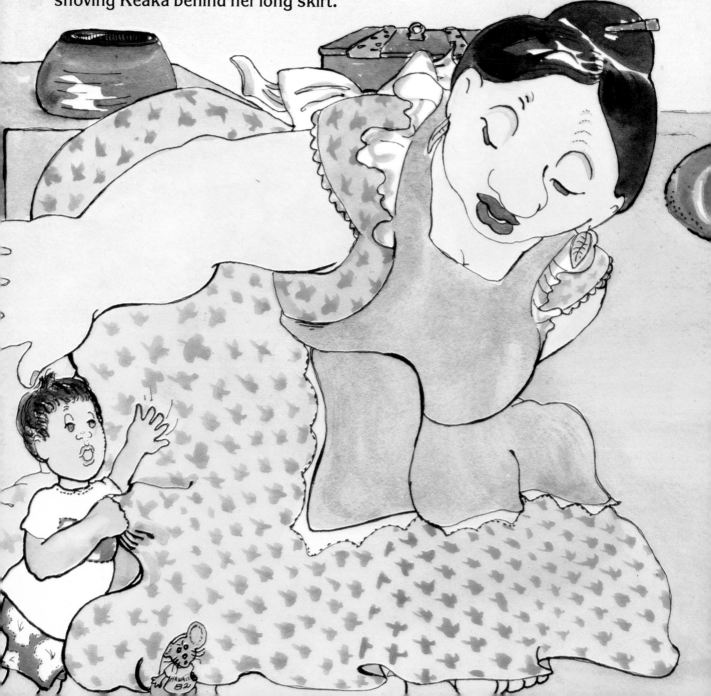

Holding tightly to the skirt, Keaka tried to hide in its folds. The rumbling grew louder and the floor began to shake. With a crash-bang, the door opened and the husband was in the house. Keaka peered fearfully from behind the wife. A giant . . . the husband was a big ugly giant.

"Wife," he said in a voice that roared. "I smell something."

"Oh dear," said the wife. "It must be your supper. I cooked laulau. Or maybe it is the squid lu'au or the kim chee."

"No," interrupted the giant. "I smell a boy."

"A boy!" gasped the wife, clutching her apron. "Oh dear, how can you smell a boy? There are no boys around here. Come. Sit down. Eat."

"Harrumph," mumbled the giant. "A boy, I smell a boy. Be he from mauka or be he from makai, I'll chew him down to his manamana wāwae." (Keaka's toes curled and quivered.)

The wife quickly brought the giant his food, poured his milk, and then began pacing nervously around the room. Everywhere she went, Keaka went too, running and panting in his effort to stay hidden. His heart was beating wildly. Keaka was scared.

"Why do you keep walking around like that?" asked the giant sharply. "Sit down somewhere."

"Great idea, giant!" thought a hot, tired Keaka.

"Oh dear," replied the wife, stopping for a moment. "I'm waiting to clear the table."

"Harrumph . . . always rushing me," grumbled the giant, licking the last bit of food off his plate.

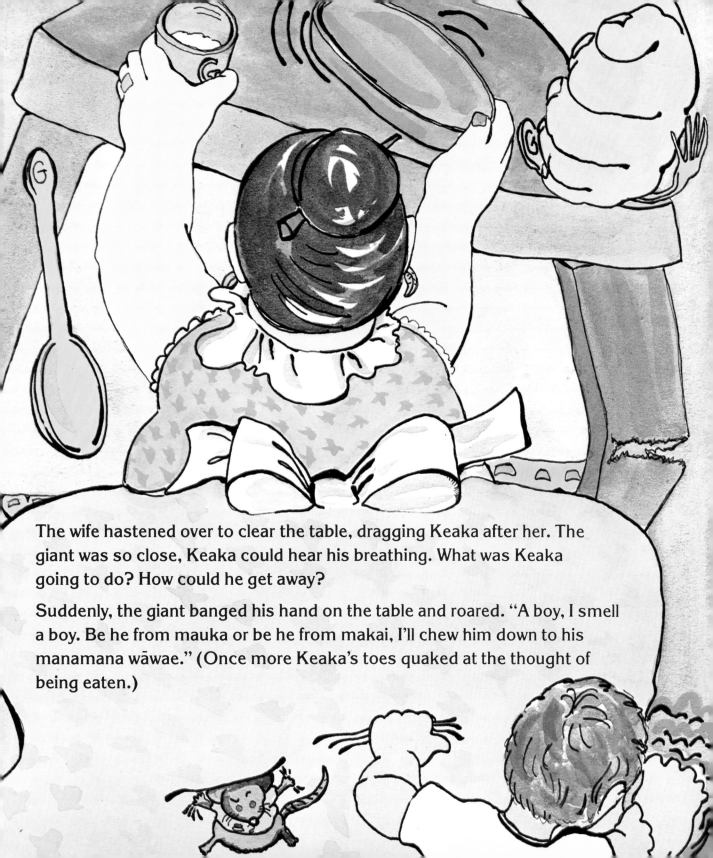

The wife hastened over to clear the table, dragging Keaka after her. The giant was so close, Keaka could hear his breathing. What was Keaka going to do? How could he get away?

Suddenly, the giant banged his hand on the table and roared. "A boy, I smell a boy. Be he from mauka or be he from makai, I'll chew him down to his manamana wāwae." (Once more Keaka's toes quaked at the thought of being eaten.)

"Oh dear," said the wife in a worried voice. "What nonsense. There is no boy around here for you to smell. Count your money, it will take your mind off of smells." Once again she began to walk and Keaka ran along behind, trying to stay out of sight.

The wife brought a large sack to the table and sat down. When all was quiet except for the giant slowly counting, "One, two, three, four," Keaka peeked out of his hiding place. He saw the giant taking coins out of the large sack. Keaka had never seen so much money before.

After counting money for awhile, the giant stood and walked across the room. He looked around and sniffed suspiciously. (How Keaka's toes shook.)

"Oh dear," said the wife, trying to catch his attention. "You must be tired after such a busy day. You created some lovely cloud shapes. And when you played ʻulu maika, the thunder you made was spectacular. Get your nēnē and ʻukulele, they will soothe and relax you."

The giant turned his back. In a flash, the wife picked Keaka up, stuffed him into a calabash, and dropped a piece of kapa over his head. With a quiet sigh of relief, Keaka sat down and listened.

The giant's feet clumped loudly as he lumbered back to the table. He said, "Harrumph," and his chair groaned as he sat down. The giant seemed to have forgotten Keaka; carefully the boy lifted the edge of the kapa and looked out.

The giant was stroking the back of a brown nēnē goose and nodding his head to a happy tune. Keaka's eyes grew big with surprise. Beside the nēnē goose were beautiful golden eggs and the tune was coming from an 'ukulele, playing by itself.

Keaka remembered the ha'i mo'olelo chanting a mele about a nēnē goose who could lay golden eggs and a magic 'ukulele that played by itself. For years they had been the prized possessions of Keaka's village. Long ago, during a fierce battle, a giant carrying a large club had taken them away.

"It isn't just a story," thought Keaka in excitement. "The giant must have kept my village's treasures all these years."

He settled back down in his hiding place, amazed at what he had discovered. For a while, the only sounds in the house were the soft cry of the nēnē goose and the music of the 'ukulele. It played songs about land shells, rainbows, and sassy little mynah birds.

All of a sudden, Keaka heard a loud snort and growl. His heart gave a jump. He began to shake. The snorting and growling grew softer and then louder and then softer once more. Keaka looked out from under the kapa again. The giant was asleep in his chair snoring.

After watching for a few minutes, Keaka climbed slowly and cautiously out of the calabash onto the table. Nearby, the wife was also sleeping. Quietly, very quietly, Keaka dropped off the table and tiptoed away. As he reached the door, he looked back at the treasures.

Tiptoeing very carefully, Keaka went back into the room and up to the sleeping giant. He gently took the nēnē goose and the ʻukulele. He tried to pick up the sack of money, but it was too heavy, he had to leave it behind.

Keaka smiled as he silently moved towards the door once more. He would take the nēnē goose and the ʻukulele to his mother. This time surely she would be pleased with what he brought home.

Out of the door Keaka crept. Swiftly down the path he ran to the vine sticking through the clouds. As he grabbed the vine, the goose, tucked tightly under his arm, let out an awful squawk.

The giant awakened, leaped to his feet, and bellowed, "A boy! A boy has taken my nēnē goose and 'ukulele. Stop boy, stop!"

The clouds rocked at the sound of his angry voice. He yelled, "A boy, be he from mauka or be he from makai, I'll chew him down to his manamana wāwae." (This time Keaka's toes were too busy to shiver or quake.)

Keaka began climbing down the vine. Down, down, down he went through the clouds towards home. The air shook with the noise of the giant.

The vine swayed as the giant too began climbing downwards. Keaka slipped and slid and climbed as fast as he could. (His frightened toes led the way, clinging to the vine.)

When Keaka was close to the bottom, he yelled. "Mother, mother, bring my cane knife! Bring my cane knife! Wiki wiki!"

At last, swinging down on a curly piece of the vine, Keaka landed beside his mother. He handed her the nēnē goose and the 'ukulele, grabbed the cane knife, and began chopping.

He could see the giant's large feet coming down the vine. He could hear the giant's booming voice getting louder and louder as he drew nearer and nearer. "A boy! When I catch a boy, be he from mauka or be he from makai, I'll chew him down to his manamana wāwae." (Oh, how Keaka's toes wished he would chop faster.)

Then with a loud crack, the knife's work was complete. The vine thundered to the ground, carrying the giant with it. As they landed, dust, dried grasses, and lava rocks rose in the air. Afterwards, all Keaka and the villagers found was a large hole. The giant was gone. Some said he bounced off into space and others said he went to the middle of the earth. But, wherever that giant went, he was never heard from again.

The wife continued to live in the white world above the earth. She learned to shape clouds and to make thunder with ʻulu maika stones. There was a large sack of money for her to spend and the giant was no longer around to worry about. She stopped saying, "Oh dear," and wringing her hands and was very content indeed.

Keaka and his mother kept the nēnē goose. The money from the golden eggs made it possible for them and all the people of their village to eat, buy new boats, and live a better life.

The magic ʻukulele was passed from family to family. Its music was so cheerful, the villagers couldn't help but live happily ever after.

# GLOSSARY
## —words as appear in book

KA'U district on the southeast side of the Island of Hawaii, the Big Island.

LAVA rock made by a volcano. Hot or cold, it is called lava.

KIAWE mesquite tree, common in Hawaii, grows well in dry areas.

KEAKA Hawaiian version of the name Jack.

'OPIHI shallow cone shaped limpet whose meat is excellent eating.

WANA an eatable spiney sea urchin.

LIMU general name for all plants living in water, in this case, a seaweed to eat.

KŪNĀNĀ Hawaiian for goat, also means puzzled.

LILIKO'I member of the passion fruit family whose fruit is used for juice and jelly.

MANAMANA WĀWAE manamana means finger. wawae means foot or leg. Together they say "finger of foot" or toes.

LAULAU pork, beef, salted fish and taro leaves wrapped in ti or banana leaves and steamed or baked.

KIM CHEE spicy Korean pickled vegetables.

SQUID LU'AU dish where squid, taro leaves (called lu'au), and coconut milk are cooked together. (Rootstalk of taro plant to be made into poi.)

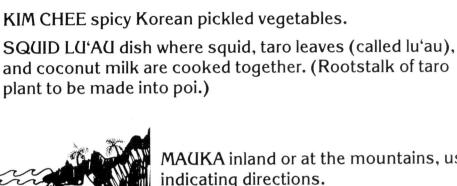

MAUKA inland or at the mountains, used in indicating directions.

MAKAI towards the ocean or at the sea, also used in giving directions.

'ULU MAIKA stone used in ancient Hawaiian bowling game called maika.

NĒNĒ species of goose living only in Hawaii. It is found on Hawaii, Maui, and at the Honolulu Zoo.

'UKULELE four stringed instrument played by strumming. Its name means "jumping flea".

HA'I MO'OLELO Ha'i means to tell. Mo'olelo means story. Together they mean storyteller.

MELE song or chant. Hawaiian stories are often related in songs and chants.

CALABASH container made from the fruit of the calabash tree; a type of gourd.

KAPA also called tapa. Cloth made by pounding the bark of wauke or mamaki plants.

WIKI hurry, quickly. WIKI WIKI means to hurry doubly fast!
PAU—FINISHED—PAU—ALL DONE—PAU—THE END!